YA GOTTA OUTMANUEVER 'EM

A TIMMY DENNISON SHORT STORY

BY TOM BEAUDIN

YA GOTTA OUTMANUEVER 'EM

A TIMMY DENNISON SHORT STORY

BY TOM BEAUDIN

Bladensburg, Maryland

YA GOTTA OUTMANUEVER 'EM

Published by
Inscript Books
a division of Dove Christian Publishers
P.O. Box 611
Bladensburg, MD 20710-0611
www.dovechristianpublishers.com

Cover Design by Barrie Lamothe

ISBN: 978-1-957497-12-9

Printed in the United States of America

To Marlene, Laura, Jason, and Adam:
Family - the gift that keeps on giving

Preface

As I write the preface to the third book in the Timmy series, we are in the midst of the 2021 Christmas season. I marvel at how, during this season, people transform into kinder, gentler versions of their rest-of-the-year selves. Christians and non-Christians alike look forward to, embrace, and bask in this annual celebration. The last Thanksgiving drumstick is yet to be consumed when Christmas decorations, accompanied by familiar Christmas melodies, miraculously appear in homes and shopping plazas across the land. Even the recent ubiquitous greeting, “Happy Holidays,” conjured up years ago to placate the PC crowd, is finding a backseat to the traditional “Merry Christmas.” After all, it is the birth of Christ that is being celebrated!

How does one account for this phenomenon? Two plausible explanations come to mind. The first revolves around the Christmas Advent wreath. Stemming from religious traditions dating back to the sixteenth century, the advent wreath is steeped in symbolism related to the birth of the Christ Child. Central in the symbolism are the five candles that are ceremoniously lighted on the four Sundays of Advent and on Christmas Eve; the first four candles represent hope, faith, joy, and peace. A fifth candle, sometimes called "the candle of love," is the Christ candle and is lighted on Christmas Eve. In a less-than-perfect world, I suspect any honest person would admit to having feelings or thoughts at one time or another of hope, faith, joy, peace, and love. To have those emotions boldly presented as a group at a given time in the calendar year offers an internal and an external excitement unseen at any other time of the year.

There is a second and perhaps more meaningful explanation for the appeal of the Christmas Season. Likely more subtle, but no less significant than the first, is the anticipation of social gatherings and, more importantly, family events wrapped up in the giving, receiving, and celebrating of the season. The concept of family dates back as far as Adam and Eve. Some would even submit that the perfect relationships within the triune Godhead suggest family perfection. The Christmas Season, in so many ways, revolves around family. First and foremost, we celebrate that little family of Mary, Joseph, and their Newborn Son, who would become the Promise of Salvation for mankind. But in a less religious sense, for many, family provides the major excitement of the season as gatherings of folks from near and far provide occasions to share memories, gifts, and updates when young and old unite with loved ones. For those without blood family or those with broken family ties, there are a variety of social and "replacement" families more than willing to fill the void. Welcoming church families, work and business families, twelve-step families, etc., sponsor and promote special events that foster the unique sense of family.

Sadly, recent years have seen the deterioration of the American "nuclear family." With that deterioration, we've experienced a loss of one of the critical building blocks necessary for a flourishing society. A strong and stable family provides for the physical and emotional needs of developing children. Religion and spirituality, as well as mutual dependence, love, trust, protection, independence, respect, and self-worth, are but some of the human needs fulfilled by a strong family unit.

Ya Gotta Outmaneuver 'Em is the third publication in the Timmy Dennison Series. It centers on the concepts of faith and trust in God's loving concern for us and our problems. Timmy Books are all about God and family. Through the experiences of a strong God-centered family unit that includes loving grandparents, the Dennison family stories offer critical spiritual concepts that are explored and hopefully resolved at a youthful level of understanding; each book embraces those aspects of family and spiritual growth that exemplify fundamental Christian living. Timmy is not the perfect child, and there is no intent to make him out to be one. Certainly, he and his family experience the normal disagreements, mishaps, and sibling rivalry of family life. In Timmy Books, though, each storyline presents a brief snippet of positive family and spiritual growth in Timmy's life. As a result, the melodrama of family arguments and wrongdoings is minimized so as not to detract from the theme of Christian family unity. In these stories, you can enjoy the mutual love of a boy and his grandparents, experience a simple answer to questions like, "What is prayer?", hear a fundamental explanation of our God-given free will, and understand other theological concepts that, if not resolved in youth, could become major obstacles to religious depth in adulthood. Timmy Books offer glimpses of a young life built on faith and trust in God, as well as a family unified by that same faith and trust. As Timmy and his family emulate the very values showcased by that Holy Family in Bethlehem some two thousand years ago, it is our prayer that America will once again embrace a return to complete and God-inspired families and that we will experience the restoration of a once-great family-centered society.

Galatians 5:22-23a

But the fruit of the Spirit is
love, joy, peace, patience,
kindness, goodness,
faithfulness, gentleness, and
self-control.

Chapter 1

The New Kids

As the principal left the classroom and closed the door, Mrs. Addison, flanked on either side by the twins, turned to the fifth-grade class and asked for their attention. "I'd like to introduce you all to two new students. Jessica Billings and her twin brother, Jeff, recently moved with their second-grade brother, Josh, and their parents to Wynhope. For the past few weeks, the children have been commuting to their former school, but as of this morning, they are attending Wynhope Elementary School, and we are privileged to have Jess and Jeff join our class. I'm certain that you will make them feel welcome."

Timmy carefully studied the two new students. *Hard to believe they're twins,* he thought. *He's a head taller than she is, and they don't look at all alike.* Timmy's mom had always cautioned him about relying on first impressions and jumping to conclusions, yet he couldn't help but wonder what Jeff's interests might be. He couldn't quite make the connection, but Jeff sure reminded him of someone. Jeff was the tallest boy in Timmy's class; in fact, he looked like he could be in seventh or eighth grade. He appeared to be quite muscular; Timmy figured that Jeff outweighed him by at least thirty pounds. Jeff looked to be all business as he walked with a bit of a swagger and ambled over to a desk that was two rows to Timmy's right.

Jessica, on the other hand, smiled at everyone as if she had known them for years. Unlike her brother, she was very thin—tiny, actually. But she was kind of cute, with obvious dimples and a heart-warming smile. As she made her way from Mrs. Addison's desk to an empty desk toward the back of the room, it was evident that she walked with a bit of a limp.

Timmy's class of 20—now 22—was a bit girl-lopsided in that there were now fourteen girls and eight boys. Not that there was anything wrong with girls, but at this point in his life,

Timmy just wasn't interested in the things most girls were interested in. Timmy loved baseball; he read baseball; he studied baseball; he talked baseball. None of the other boys in his class were particularly sports-minded, and although Timmy got along with all of them, he seldom interacted with any of them outside of school.

About the only thing that interrupted Timmy's baseball world was his fascination and skill with flying remote-control helicopters. Prompted by a Christmas gift from his Gram & Gramp when he was eight years old, he had developed a keen interest in flying and had spent hours developing skills while learning some of the basic flying stunts he had seen on YouTube. He hadn't done much flying of late, primarily because his best technician, repairman, critic, fan, and beloved Gramp was now flying in heaven with the angels.

Gramp had died suddenly the previous summer, and his death had left a huge hole in Timmy's life. Timmy's family dynamics were such that he spent a lot of time with his recently widowed maternal grandmother, who lived just three houses away on the same street where Timmy and his family lived. Timmy's dad taught at the middle school; his mom spent a lot of time volunteering at St. Alban's Hospital; his older sister, Lindy, was a sophomore at college, and his brother, Matt, was a senior at Wynhope High. Matt was an all-around athlete who excelled in basketball. Although he hadn't played baseball in his junior year, he was a sure bet to lock up this year's third base spot.

As a result, most school days found Timmy stopping to visit with his beloved Gram rather than going home to an empty house. He confided in her during many of those visits, sharing his successes and failures and always opening his heart and mind to her God-given wisdom. After Gramp died, Timmy took on some of Gramp's chores so that Gram could remain cared for in the home that she had shared with Gramp since way before Timmy was born. Though Timmy dearly loved his Gram, he sorely missed his Gramp, and there was always a sense of closeness and peace when he did some of Gramp's chores or worked in Gramp's workshop.

Timmy continued sizing up Jeff and imagined him playing on Timmy's Little League team in the coming weeks and months. *Bet he could hit that ball outta the park,* thought Timmy. *I wonder if he's a lefty or a righty.* His imagination took off, and in the next few minutes, Timmy saw the entire season develop as this new student-turned-baseball star single-handedly hit the team to a 15-0 season record. He was so deep in thought that he didn't even notice an older student enter the classroom, speak quietly to Mrs. Addison, and leave the room. He was planning how he would meet Jeff and convince him to join baseball tryouts next week when suddenly...

"Timmy Dennison, are you listening to me?" scolded Mrs. Addison.

Timmy snapped back to reality.

"I just received a message from the main office student helper. You are to report immediately to the principal's office."

As Mrs. Addison's words slowly sank in, Timmy cautiously got up from his desk and headed toward the classroom door. He failed to see the surprised concern on Aaron Wilson's face.

1Peter 5:7

Cast all your anxiety on Him
because He cares for you.

Chapter 2

The Scare

In all his years in school, Timmy had never been summoned to the principal's office. Of course, he had heard stories from those who had, and given the exaggerations of his classmates, he approached the school office with a good amount of caution and fear. Upon entering the office, he noticed that his mom was sitting on the "in trouble" bench — that infamous bench where students sat while waiting to be seen by Miss Ludwig, the principal. He sat next to his mom and asked her what was going on. "I'll let Miss Ludwig explain," she said curtly.

About five minutes later, Miss Ludwig appeared and invited them into her office. After everyone was seated, Miss Ludwig began. "Timmy, I received a call this morning from Mr. Wadkins, the owner of Wadkins Sporting Goods in the center of town. Were you there yesterday afternoon after school?"

"Yes, I was," responded Timmy. "Mom and Dad had given me permission to ride my bike to school and to stop there on my way home so that I could buy a roll of grip tape for my baseball bat."

"Well," continued Miss Ludwig, "apparently, sometime after you left the store, someone called Mr. Wadkins and told him that they had seen a customer slip a pair of $25 Lizard Skins batting gloves into their bookbag and leave the store without paying. Mr. Watkins told me he had checked his computer and found that the pair of Lizard Skins was the last in his inventory and was indeed missing."

The blood drained from Timmy's face, and tears welled up in his eyes. He tried to speak, but nothing would come out. He turned to his mother and said, "Mom ... I ... uh ... I don't ... uh ... I can't ..." And that was it; he just had no words. His mind was blank.

Miss Ludwig continued. "Mr. Wadkins called the school here because he didn't want to involve the police. He gave me a list of several Wynhope students who frequent his store. I will be speaking with each of those students. He did say that he understood how these things happen, are sometimes part of growing up, and that he would be satisfied to either get the gloves back or to receive payment for them." The resulting silence was deafening.

Gradually, as Timmy calmed a bit, he was finally able to speak. He wiped the tears from his eyes and turned to his mom. "Mom, I didn't steal anything. I swear I didn't. When I got to the store, I was kinda in a hurry 'cause I had told Gram that I would stop by after school and help her rotate the mattress on her bed. So, I parked my bike, threw my bookbag over the handlebars, and went in to see what kinds of grip tape Mr. Watkins might have. Don't you see? I couldn't have slipped the gloves into my bookbag, 'cause I didn't bring my bookbag into the store when I went in."

Miss Ludwig looked at Timmy with a sour face and exclaimed, "Timmy! What if someone had stolen your schoolbooks while you were in the store?"

Get real, lady, thought Timmy. *Like someone is really going to steal a bunch of fifth-grade textbooks.*

Timmy's mom smiled, turned to Miss Ludwig, and said, "I assume that we are done here. I appreciate your calling me and inviting me to be here for this conference. Timmy will not be returning to class today; I will be taking him home with me, and I assure you that we will straighten things out with Mr. Wadkins." With that, she grabbed Timmy by the hand, left the office, and headed for the parking lot.

Fortunately, there were no customers in Mr. Wadkins's store when Timmy and his mom arrived. They walked up to the check-out counter, where Mr. Wadkins was busy re-arranging the display. "May I help you?" he asked.

Timmy stepped forward and said, "Hi, Mr. Wadkins. Do you remember me?"

"Of course I do, young man. You were in the other day and bought some grip tape for your 28-inch Easton Beast baseball bat. How did you make out re-wrapping the handle? Everything go OK?"

"My dad helped me," said Timmy. "Everything worked good. But that's not why we're here. This morning, my school principal called me and my mom to her office. She told us that you had called her about some stolen batting gloves. I want you to know that I didn't steal anything, Mr. Wadkins. Honest! Miss Ludwig—she's my principal—said that the person who called you claimed that someone put the gloves in their bookbag, but it couldn't have been me, Mr. Wadkins, 'cause when I came in, I left my bookbag on my bike outside the store on account of it had so many books in it; it was too heavy to lug around." With that, he took a breath and looked pleadingly at Mr. Wadkins.

Mr. Wadkins smiled, pointed to a video camera high on the wall behind him, and said, "First of all, the person who called never mentioned anyone by name. They simply said it was 'one of my customers.' After I spoke with Miss Ludwig, I checked the video footage and clearly saw that you did not have a bookbag with you. I also looked to see if anyone else was in the store, but the camera angle didn't show anyone. I am terribly sorry for any inconvenience that this may have caused you. I will call Miss Ludwig and gladly clear your name."

Timmy and his mom thanked Mr. Wadkins and left the store for home.

Job 2:11

When Job's three friends, Eliphaz the Temanite, Bildad the Shuhite, and Zophar the Naamathite, heard about all the troubles that had come upon him, they set out from their homes and met together by agreement to go and sympathize with him and comfort him.

Chapter 3

Job's Lesson

Later that same evening, Timmy sat with his mom and dad and expressed his frustration at the events of the day. He was hurt that he had been suspected of stealing and confused that God would allow such a thing to happen. In fact, he found himself actually blaming God for his misfortune. And to make matters worse, it embarrassed him to have been called from the classroom to the office. He was also upset about the thought of having to face his classmates.

After Timmy had vented his frustrations, his mom was the first to speak. "Many years ago," she began, "when I was just about your age, my best friend told a lie about me, and I was pretty upset — just as you are today. Gramp, in all his wisdom, let me stew about it for a few days before he sat me down and read with me the story of Job. Have you ever read the Book of Job?"

"I've never read it," answered Timmy, "but we have talked about it in Sunday School, and I know that one of the characters in the story is the smallest dude in all of Scripture."

After a moment's pause, Dad said, "OK, I'll bite. Who was 'the smallest dude in all of Scripture?'"

With a satisfied grin, Timmy answered, "One of Job's friends was Bildad, the Shuhite."

Mom chuckled and then continued, "OK. Can we get serious for a minute? You're understandably upset. I'm guessing that at least part of your being upset is that God allowed the accusation to even take place. Now, I'm sure you remember our talk a while back when Matt asked us to pray for his friend Walter, who had been making some bad choices. When I sat with Gramp all those years ago, he reminded me that a lot of things that happen, both good and bad, result from God's gift of free will. Theologians often refer to it as 'God's permissive will.' In the Book of Job, we read how Satan, making use of

God's permissive will, tested Job by destroying his livestock, his possessions, his wealth, and his family. Yet, through unwavering faith and trust, Job recognized God's omnipotence and didn't blame God; rather, he tried to understand God's will and held strong to his trust in God. Job knew that God does not bring about evil; rather, He is the solution to the problem of evil and the remedy for every pain we suffer."

Dad had been listening intently and watched for Timmy's reaction as Mom had relayed some of the key lessons from the Book of Job. Finally, he interrupted. "You know, Timmy, in the story, three of Job's friends go to visit him after all the disasters. Why do you think that his three friends, Eliphaz the Temanite, Zophar the Naamathite, and 'Stretch' got together and went to meet with Job?"

"Probably to get all the gory details from him," answered Timmy.

"Not true," said Dad. "They went so that they could sympathize with him and give him comfort and support. So, if the story of the theft at Mr. Wadkins's store is 'out there,' and that's a big 'if,' I'm inclined to think that your classmates will try to comfort and support you. Since you did nothing wrong, I wouldn't think that you have cause to be embarrassed."

"Dad, you just don't know what fifth grade is like today. Everybody knows everybody else's business, and the school gossip is worse than the gossip at Gram's knitting club." Timmy paused for a moment and then added, "Last week, when we were studying the second World War, Mrs. Addison was telling us about Winston Churchill, Britain's Prime Minister during the war. She read from a book of quotes some of his famous lines. One of those quotes that he is known to have used, although apparently others before him are thought to have used it also, is, 'A lie gets halfway around the world before the truth has a chance to get its pants on.' That just about describes fifth grade at Wynhope."

"Well," said Mom, "let's wait and see what tomorrow brings. There's no sense worrying about something that hasn't even happened yet. Paul's letter to the Romans mentions the assurance we have that God will work everything out. Perhaps later on tonight, you can check out Romans 8:28. It might strengthen your faith and trust that God will work this out with you. Right now, maybe it's time you got started on your homework."

As Timmy headed to his room, his brother, Matt, was on his way to the living room to watch an NHL game with Dad. Although he starred in basketball and baseball, there wasn't a sport that he didn't watch when time and homework allowed. "Hey Timmy, wait up a sec. I gotta show ya something."

Apparently, the father of Danny, one of Matt's friends, was one of the adults who coached and managed the Little League. Sign-ups had recently taken place for tryouts a couple of weeks away. Those who had been previously drafted to one of the five teams remained on those teams, but as a service to the coaches, the league compiled a list of those new candidates who had signed up for tryouts and would be eligible for this year's draft. The list was supposed to be confidential until after tryouts were complete but usually became general knowledge long before it was supposed to. Matt took out his cell phone, thumbed through his pictures until he found the one he wanted, and said to Timmy, "Check this out. But remember, you didn't see it from me." The pic had been sent to him by his friend Danny and was of the list of potential new players. The fourth name from the top was *J. Billings*.

Luke 6:37

Do not judge and you will not be judged. Do not condemn, and you will not be condemned. Forgive and you will be forgiven.

Chapter 4

Forgiveness

Timmy finished his homework, bid his parents a good night, said his evening prayers, and climbed into bed. With thoughts of a powerhouse team behind the imagined skills of this giant of a student who looked like the Little League's coming of the new Babe Ruth, Timmy fell into a deep and satisfying sleep, confident that the earlier events of the day were mercifully in his rearview mirror.

The next day, Friday, was a teacher in-service day, giving Timmy a much-cherished day off from school. He already knew that he would spend part of the day helping Gram. He intended to keep his promise to help her rotate her mattress, and he suspected that there might be a few other things that he could help her with. Dad had to be at school, and Matt had a morning practice for the end-of-season league tournament, so they were out of the house by 8:00.

At 10:00, Mom was scheduled to be at St. Alban's Hospital nursery, where she volunteered several mornings a week. "I know you offered to help Gram," she said to Timmy. "How about we leave together around 9:30, and I can drop you off? It'll give me a few minutes to visit with Gram."

Of course, Gram was delighted to see them. She was slowly recovering from the sudden loss of Gramp and was gradually getting back to a more normal routine. For several months after Gramp's death, she had been overcome with loneliness and was only now showing signs of emotional recovery. Still, she missed Gramp terribly; she would always miss him. But her church family had stepped up, Timmy and his family had tried to include her in their everyday lives, and her strong faith and trust in God had provided much necessary healing. She and Mom chatted for a few minutes while Timmy disappeared to the cellar to Gramp's workshop. Sitting on the floor was Timmy's helo, right where Gramp had left it after the last repair. Timmy hadn't flown it since Gramp's death. He said it was because if it crashed, he wouldn't have anyone to help with repairs. This was, of course, partially true, but if the entire truth be told, Gramp had always been part of the flying routine. Timmy had never flown alone, and he just wasn't ready to make this great adjustment and go on without Gramp there. *Maybe today's the day,* thought Timmy. *The sun is warm, the air is thin and light, and there's no wind.*

After Mom left, Timmy and Gram went to the bedroom to flip and rotate the mattress on her queen bed. The mattress was one of those big thick ones, and Timmy could readily see why this was a two-person job. First, they rotated it 90 degrees clockwise and then another 90 degrees clockwise. Then they flipped it so that the head was now at the foot and vice versa. When Gram was remaking the bed, the bottom sheet caught on the bed frame and caused a pretty large rip in the sheet. They finished the process, and Gram made a mental note to replace the sheets. They adjourned to the kitchen table and a well-earned snack. Gram had baked an apple pie earlier in the week, and she carved out a generous piece, placed it on a plate, and topped it with a spoonful of Cool

Whip. She made herself a cup of tea and sat at the table, where Timmy was already well into polishing off the piece of pie.

"So," began Gram, "I hear you had a pretty exciting day yesterday."

"I'm not sure that 'exciting' is the word I would use," responded Timmy. "Sure were a lot of 'firsts,' though. First time I ever got called to the principal's office; first time Mom ever got called to the principal's office; first time I was ever suspected of stealing... I was really bummed out. Yep, 'bummed out' is a better description than 'exciting.' I think Mr. Wadkins and I have it pretty much straightened out, though. Thank God for video cameras. Trouble is, the camera didn't show who actually stole the gloves. Probably just as well; if I ever got my hands on the culprit, he or she would be one hurtin' dude."

"'Vengeance is mine,' said The Lord" was Gram's response.

"What the heck is that supposed to mean?" asked Timmy.

"Actually," said Gram, "there's more to the saying than that. Deuteronomy 32:35 quotes the Lord, Who says, in part, 'It is mine to avenge. I will repay.' Pretty much, we're reminded in several areas of Scripture that the judgment of a person's heart belongs to the Lord and only the Lord. We can never know all the circumstances that are involved in a person's thoughts and actions, and that is why it's not ours to judge. If you really want to do something, there is a good piece of advice in Proverbs 25:21,22. 'If your enemy is hungry, feed him; if he is thirsty, give him something to drink. In doing this, you will heap burning coals on his head.' Bottom line is that God doesn't want you planning to get even. All that will ever accomplish is to make a bitter and angry person more bitter and more angry."

"Well, if I could just get them back," said Timmy, "I'd feel a lot better."

Gram sternly responded, "Now you listen to me, young man; that's not how it works!"

Oops! Timmy bolted upright in his chair. Gram had never raised her voice to him, and he had a shocked look that made her soften a bit.

"This whole issue is about forgiveness," she said. "Scripture is so very clear on the topic of forgiveness." Grabbing her Bible off the counter, she said, "Let's start with the Gospel of Matthew. In chapter 6, we read about the time that Jesus answered a request from the apostles about how they should pray. He taught them what has become known as 'The Lord's Prayer.' In that prayer, He directed, 'Forgive us our debts as we also have forgiven our debtors.' A couple of verses later, He added, 'for if you forgive men when they sin against you, your heavenly Father will also forgive you. But if you do not forgive their sins, your Father will not forgive your sins.' Can't get much clearer than that!"

"I get it," responded Timmy. "I'm supposed to forgive. But I'm not even sure how to do that. How can I ever forget the trouble this person has caused me?"

Gram thought for a moment and then said, "Well, to begin with, forgiving doesn't mean forgetting; it *does* mean giving up the anger and the resolve to 'pay someone back.' It doesn't mean that you will like the person, but it *does* mean that you will love the person. Basically, it means that you will let God deal with it and with you. When you forgive someone, you're not restoring their heart; you're restoring your own. Think about this. If you do something wrong or sin against God, you will probably be unsettled in your heart and soul. You may not even realize it, but you wouldn't feel quite right. Now, if you then stood before God with your sin, what would you ask of Him?"

Timmy thought for a moment before answering. "Well, first, I'd probably tell Him all the reasons why I think He should let me off the hook for what I did."

"In other words, you'd make up a lot of excuses."

"Well, I guess you could say that. Then, I think I'd probably say to Him, 'C'mon, God, go easy on me. You can't hold this little thing against me for the rest of my life. How about you give me a pass this time and let me go forward with a clean slate?'"

"And that's exactly what He would do, and that's exactly what you are called to do for someone else."

"I don't know if I can do that," said Timmy. "I'm not God, you know."

"You don't have to be; just ask Him for help. He is always there."

There was a long moment of silence before Timmy spoke. "Thanks, Gram. You always know how to make the hurt go away. Sorry I can be such a pain sometimes."

Gram smiled. "There is one more thing," she added. "Part of forgiveness is that whenever possible, you should tell the offender that you forgive them."

"Why?"

"First of all," Gram responded, "the person may not even know that they have offended you, so telling them you forgive them alerts them they've possibly done something offensive. But more importantly, when you tell someone that you forgive them, you are making a commitment, a commitment to them, a commitment to yourself, and a commitment to God. Kinda hard to back out of all those commitments."

Gram stood, picked up the empty pie dish, and placed it in the sink. She turned around, put her arms around Timmy, who had gotten up from his chair, and said, "It's been a while since we've had a talk like this. I hope I've helped you; I know I've helped myself. Sometimes, I just miss your Gramp so much, and when you and I talk, I see so much of him in you. Well, it soothes my loneliness and settles my heart."

"I'm the lucky one," responded Timmy. He paused before continuing. "You know, Gram, I haven't flown the helo since Gramp went to heaven. Somehow, it just wasn't right to fly without him. But I can't not fly for the rest of my life. I think he'd want me to fly again, and I think today's as good a day as any. Would it be OK to take the helo out back and check things out?"

"It's certainly OK with me. I'm gonna run to the store and get a set of sheets to replace the one that got ripped earlier today. You don't need me while you're flying, but do be careful. And, if you leave for home before I get back, don't forget to lock up the house."

Timmy hugged Gram, kissed her goodbye, and went to the cellar to get the helo. As he headed back outside, his heart was thumping with the excitement of flying once again. Today would be different because Gramp wouldn't be beside him, but Timmy felt him nearby, and he knew that Gramp was with him in spirit.

Zechariah 7:9

This is what The Lord, Almighty says: “Administer true justice; show mercy and compassion to one another.”

Chapter 5

Mr. W. to the Rescue

In another part of town, Timmy's classmate, Aaron Wilson, was in a panic. His mom, who had recently been diagnosed with type 2 diabetes, was showing signs of hypoglycemia. Three months ago, Aaron wouldn't have been able to pronounce the word, let alone recognize its signs and give first aid for it. His mom and her doctor had been struggling with the right balance of the best diabetic diet, including eating regularly and adequate insulin intake.

Aaron and his mom lived alone, just three-quarters of a mile from the center of Wynhope.

Aaron was an only child whose father had been killed in an auto accident when Aaron was only five. As a result, Aaron and his mom were very close. Aaron had grown up fast after his dad died, and since his mom's diabetes diagnosis, he had become quite protective of her. Fortunately, she shared everything that she knew about the disease with him.

This was not the first hypoglycemic event in recent weeks, and Aaron knew exactly what to do. His mom was already a bit disoriented, so he helped her to the living room sofa where she could rest while he got her a glass of orange juice. He then went to the kitchen, got a glass from the cupboard, and opened the refrigerator door to grab the container of orange juice. Oops! Aaron suddenly remembered that he had finished the juice that had been in the refrigerator. He ran back to the living room, sat next to his mom, and said, "Mom, I goofed. I drank the remaining OJ earlier today. You stay right here. I'm gonna go to the Food Mart and get some more OJ, and I'll be right back."

With that, he jumped on his bike and peddled as fast as he could to the Food Mart, just three-quarters of a mile away. It wasn't until he was almost there that he realized that he hadn't taken any money with him. He and his mom didn't usually shop at the Food Mart, and consequently, they didn't know anyone there. Aaron was panic-stricken. On the verge of tears, he ran four doors down to Wadkins Sporting Goods. Just about everybody in town knew Mr. Wadkins, who supplied almost all the kids with their sporting needs. He was an older man with a gentle nature and could be seen at almost every sporting event in Wynhope. Often, kids would stop in the store just to chat with him or seek his advice on anything from sports to homework. Aaron went in, found Mr. Wadkins in the back, and told him about his dilemma.

Without hesitation, Mr. Wadkins ran to the phone and called the Food Mart. "Hi, this is Clint Wadkins," he began. "I'm sending a young man to you; he'll be there in a matter of minutes. Give him whatever he needs and put the cost of the items on my bill." With that, he rushed Aaron out the door. Aaron ran back to the Food Mart, identified himself, grabbed a half-gallon of fresh orange juice, showed it to the clerk, jumped on his bike, and was home in no time. He threw down his bike, ran into the house, poured a glass of juice, and brought it to his mom. Within minutes, she felt better.

Aaron gingerly sat on the sofa next to his mom. "Mom," he began, "I got almost all the way to the Food Mart when I realized that I hadn't brought any money. Luckily, Mr. Wadkins was in his store, and when I told him what was going on, he called the Food Mart and instructed them to put whatever I needed on his bill. The amount was $6.15."

"Well, I'll be going into town later this afternoon; I will be sure to pay him and thank him for his kindness. We are so lucky to have him here in town."

Aaron continued. "That's not what I wanted to tell you, though. Wednesday, when I stopped at the hardware store to get your drapery brackets, something funny happened that's kinda been bothering me."

"What's that, dear?"

"Well, when I left the store, I ran into Timmy Dennison as he was leaving Wadkins Sporting. We said 'Hi' to each other, talked about school for a minute or so, and then he hustled off for home. Right after he left, an older boy stopped me and asked me who it was that I was just talking to. He said something about how he'd seen him drop an item and wanted to return it to him. I told him Timmy's name but thought afterward that I probably shouldn't have done that. Then yesterday, Timmy got called to the office and never returned to class. What do you think I should do?"

"You'll get a chance to talk to Timmy in school on Monday, so for now, don't worry about it. I'm sure it's OK."

Psalm 34:7

The angel of The Lord encamps around those who fear Him, and He delivers them.

Chapter 6

Gabriel

"OK, Gramp, let's see if I can still remember everything." Timmy talked to Gramp as if Gramp were right there beside him. At first, this had concerned his parents. However, Pastor Remy, as well as the school psychologist, had assured them that this was part of Timmy's way of coping with the loss. With the passing of time, the out-loud verbal conversations would probably diminish, although Pastor Remy said that Timmy might mentally speak to Gramp for years to come. In fact, he revealed that he often mentally spoke to his mother, with whom he had been very close.

Timmy started the engines and brought the helo to a hover about three feet off the ground. He made a few basic maneuvers in order to regain his touch with the controls and then said to no apparent listener, "Let's do it." He brought the helo up to about twenty feet to check the wind currents. Satisfied, he began to fly circles just above Gram's house. With each revolution that he made, he felt more and more comfortable. Suddenly, the helo started to drop and Timmy lost control. So as not to have a runaway helo flying wildly around the neighborhood, Timmy immediately cut all power. The helo dove about ten feet and hit the roof. It slid down the rake of the roof until the tail assembly got caught in the junction of the gutter and the downspout. Timmy instinctively looked around for Gramp, but, of course, Gramp wasn't there.

Timmy was no stranger to helo accidents. But before today, Gramp had always been there to pick up the pieces and fix everything. Today was different. He collected his thoughts and headed for the shed, where Gramp kept all his outdoor tools. Inside the shed, on the right-hand side, was the fifteen-foot step ladder. Timmy struggled to free it from the surrounding tools and lugged it over to the corner of the house. *This'll be a piece of cake,* he thought as he set the ladder in position. He climbed up to the third step and could just barely touch the helo but could not unhook it from the downspout. Ignoring his dad's advice to never extend his reach from a ladder, he went up another step and reached way out ... and that was all he remembered until he woke up on the ground with a young man kneeling next to him, checking his pulse.

"Timmy, are you OK?"

It's funny what goes through your mind in those weird moments. Timmy's first thought was, *I don't know this guy; how does he know my name? I've never even seen him before.*

As if on cue, the man's next words were "Hi, my name is Gabriel; most folks call me Gabe. I was passing by, heard the commotion, and ran over to see if I could help you out."

Timmy sat up and looked around. Slowly, he pieced together what had happened. Except for his pride, only his wrist was hurt, and he was pretty sure that it was hurt bad. "Thanks," he finally mumbled. Timmy tried to stand, and Gabe reached out to help. He grabbed Timmy's hurt wrist and pulled him up. Timmy was about to scream out in pain when he suddenly realized that there was no pain. The wrist wasn't hurting anymore. The ladder was lying on the ground, and next to it was the helo with a pretty well-messed-up tail section. Timmy looked down at it, turned to Gabe, and said, "My Gramp used to fly with me, but he died recently, and this was the first time I attempted it alone. He never really helped me fly; he just fixed all my mistakes. I guess now I'll have to put into practice every repair trick he taught me."

"I'm sorry about your Gramp," said Gabe, "and sorry you crashed your helo. But if you play it right, you can usually profit from your mistakes. Mistakes almost always make for problems, and problems can always be solved. But you need to trust that God will provide solutions by giving you the insight that you might never have come up with on your own. One of my friends, when faced with all sorts of problems, always says, 'Ya gotta outmaneuver 'em,' meaning that you don't just avoid problems; instead, you work your way through those problems, inspired by God's help."

Timmy couldn't believe his ears. He had never heard anyone but Gramp use that saying.

"It boils down to this," continued Gabe. "'Ya gotta outmaneuver 'em' means that you have to use faith and trust. Faith is believing that God is Who He says He is, and trust is taking that faith and acting on the solutions that God gives you." He paused long enough for that to sink in and then continued. "Let me give you an example that might help you understand. Suppose that you're at bat and there is a runner on first base. There's one out, and the count is 2-0. Your baseball know-how leads you to believe that there's a good chance that the pitcher will try like crazy to throw a strike on the next pitch. Based on that belief, you act by setting up for an inside-out swing in order to hit behind the runner. You see? First, there's faith in your baseball knowledge, and then follows trust by acting on your belief and changing your set-up."

Just then, Gram returned from her shopping trip. She got out of the car, looked around, and took in the strange scene. She noticed the knocked-over ladder, the damaged helo, and the stranger standing next to Timmy.

Immediately, Timmy tried to defuse Gram's anticipated comments. He began by saying, "Hi Gram. Did you get the sheets that you went for?" Not giving her a chance to answer, he continued, "I had a little accident — lost control of the helo and it got caught on the downspout. I was trying to get it down when I guess I slipped off the ladder and fell. Don't worry, I'm OK. This man—his name is Gabe—was in the area, and he ran over to make sure that I wasn't hurt."

Gabe stepped forward, held out his hand, and repeated his previous introduction. "Hi, Mrs. Largent; my name is Gabriel. Most of my friends call me Gabe. I'm very pleased to meet you. I happened to be in the area, heard the commotion, and came over to make sure that Timmy was OK."

Once again, Timmy thought, *How does he know Gram's name?*

"Well, I certainly thank you, Gabe, for your help and concern." Gram paused and then continued. "I've lived here in Wynhope for years, and I'm pretty sure that I know most people in town; I don't remember seeing you around. Are you new in town?"

"No, not really; I'm just sorta passing through." Turning to Timmy, he said, "Timmy, it was great to see you *again.* Glad that I happened to be in the neighborhood. You take care of that wrist now; you're gonna need it in tip-top shape for the upcoming baseball season." With that, he turned and headed out of the driveway, turned left, and ambled down the road, whistling away as he went.

"Now, he was certainly a nice young man," said Gram.

"Gram, listen. What's that tune he's whistling?" asked Timmy.

"Sounds to me like the German Christmas Carol, *O Tannenbaum,*" answered Gram.

"Gram!" exclaimed Timmy. "Did we just meet an angel?"

"What makes you ask that?" asked Gram.

"Are you kidding me? First, he appears out of nowhere. Then he calls me by name. How'd he even know my name? In fact, how'd he even know *your* name? And speaking of names, he said his name was Gabriel. He grabbed me by my hurt wrist to help me stand, and suddenly my wrist didn't hurt anymore. Coincidence? How about when he said, 'Ya gotta outmaneuver 'em'? Did you ever hear anyone except Gramp say that? Oh, and did you catch when he said, '...it was great to see you *again*?' *Again* means that there must have been a *before*."

Abruptly changing the subject, Timmy asked Gram if she needed any help bringing packages from the car into the house. She declined his help, so he grabbed the ladder and returned it to the shed. He then picked up the damaged helo and brought it to the cellar, where he placed it on the floor next to Gramp's workbench. *In a few days,* he thought, *I'll fully check out the damage and try to figure out what went wrong.* He knew that any repair would be "iffy" but was confident in the training that

Gramp had so often provided. He returned to the kitchen, where Gram had made a nice cup of hot chocolate. They sat and talked, mostly about Gabe. Timmy continued to insist that there was just too much there to be handed off to coincidence.

"Gram, really," he persisted, "you knew Gramp a whole lot longer than I knew him. How many times in all your years together did you hear him say 'Ya gotta outmaneuver 'em'?"

"More than I could ever count," was Gram's reply. "Almost every time he was faced with a problem or successfully worked through a puzzling set of circumstances."

"And in all those years," continued Timmy, "how many other people did you ever hear use that saying?"

"None" was Gram's reply.

"And another thing," said Timmy excitedly. "How about whistling a Christmas tune in April, and one about a Christmas tree, no less? Remember me telling you about a dream I had a while back where an angel spoke to me and then appeared hovering above the town Christmas tree? Could that be the '*before*'? That was the same Christmas that me and Gramp, er, I mean Gramp and I had a pretty long discussion about angels."

"OK," said Gram. "You're pretty convincing. But why don't we just digest it all, wait and see if Gabe shows up in town anymore, and then come to grips with today's happenings?"

With that, Timmy got up from his chair, thanked Gram for the hot chocolate, gave her a kiss and a big hug, and said, "Dad left a few chores for me to do today. I think I'd better get home and get 'em done."

Off he went.

Exodus 20.8

Remember the Sabbath day
by keeping it holy.

Chapter 7

Family Day

The weekend flew by. It's funny how time affects us. Timmy wasn't exactly ready to face his classmates after what had happened on Thursday, so, of course, the time flew by. He wished it would have been a little slower. On the other hand, he anxiously awaited the Little League tryouts and team selection that would happen in about a week. For this, he wished the time to speed by. Of course, the time would drag on until tryout day. On Saturday, he went to Gram's, set the helo up on Gramp's bench, and made a list of the parts that he would need. Then he went through the spare parts that he and Gramp had collected in the past few years and checked off his list those that he found. He spent some time repairing what he could on the helo before returning home. With manuals and parts lists that he kept on his desk, he made a complete list of parts, with part numbers, that he would need to order. He would bring that list one day next week to the sporting goods store so that Mr. Wadkins could send an order to his supplier.

Sunday dawned bright and early. Sunday was church day; it was also "family" day. Timmy, Matt, and Lindy had grown up knowing that Sunday was a day for the family. After church and Sunday school, they spent the day at home, where they hung out and ate meals together. Coaches knew that the Dennison kids didn't practice and didn't do games on Sundays. Most of them readily accepted that fact; some even applauded it. In fact, Matt's basketball coach never held a Sunday practice or scheduled a Sunday game. Friends were always welcome at their home, and most of them loved being there, but they, too, knew and honored the Dennison traditions. Most Sundays, Gram would go to church with the family and then join them in whatever was planned for the rest of the day.

On this particular Sunday, Timmy caught up with Pastor Remy after Sunday school. He told him about what had happened on Friday, including his experience with Gabriel. Pastor Remy listened intently. Timmy related all the 'coincidences' of the encounter. He finished by saying, "I know that Scripture has many references to angels appearing on earth. Gramp and I had a long conversation about angels just before God called him home. We found lotsa places in the Bible that were about angels among us. But that was thousands of years ago. What about now? Do angels still visit the earth? Have you ever seen an angel? Do you know anyone who has?"

"Timmy," began Pastor Remy, "I'm so sorry, but I don't know for certain the answers to all your questions. Here's what I do know, or at least have reasoned to with my God-given brain. God created the heavens, the earth, and all that is in them. God has used angels in the past, often to deliver messages to people on earth, just as He did with Mary and Joseph. I can't think of a reason why He wouldn't use them today for the same reasons. Remember, we think in time, a day, a year, a thousand years; God has no time; for Him, everything is in the present. Consequently, when we think of what God does or doesn't do, the separation of thousands of years is somewhat meaningless. Now, as a part of my ministry, I have been with people who died in my presence. Some, just before death, had experiences of being met by loved ones who had gone before them, and some said that they were in the presence of angels. I remember one woman who sat up in bed and, for several minutes, sang with the angels who, she said, were in the room. Finally, I know of a man who swears that an angel saved him from being electrocuted. You know, God talks to the young and old alike, and He does so in a variety of ways. I often tell those who say that God never talks to them, that perhaps they're just not listening. So, let me ask you just one question. Do you believe that this Gabriel fella was an angel?"

"I do," answered Timmy with no hesitation.

"Then I suspect he was."

After Sunday dinner, the afternoon was spent in a challenging game of backyard wiffle ball. Timmy, Matt, and their dad played against three of Matt's basketball teammates. One of them, Danny, who pitched for his team, could make the wiffle ball drop, curve in, curve out, and rise from ankle level to shoulder level. Timmy had never seen such wiffle ball pitching mastery and struck out twice before finally hitting a little dribbler. Talk about being humbled! Danny and his team won 9-3.

The family spent a quiet evening watching TV and preparing for school on Monday. Timmy was actually looking forward to school, as he anticipated getting to know Jeff Billings and talking with him about Little League.

Proverbs 22:29

Do you see someone skilled in their work? They will serve before kings; they will not serve before officials of low rank.

Chapter 8

Try-outs

As soon as he got to school on Monday, Timmy looked for Jeff Billings, but both Jeff and his sister, Jessica, were absent. It wasn't until Thursday that Jessica returned to class and explained that she and her brother had been sick with the flu; she was feeling better, but Jeff still had a fever, and their mom had decided to keep him home for another day or two. Timmy still hoped that Jeff would make the tryouts and team selection.

Not once during the week was there any mention of Timmy having been called to the office on Friday. On Tuesday, Miss Ludwig visited the class and spent the better part of an hour observing the classroom atmosphere. Of course, as soon as the principal entered the room and the entire time she was there, the students were on their best behavior. Somehow, even fifth graders knew that at least part of this visit was to see how Mrs. Addison was performing as a teacher. Mrs. Addison was very much liked by her students, and in no small way, they were quite protective of her.

When Jeff didn't show up for school on Friday, Timmy was pretty certain that he probably wouldn't be at tryouts on Saturday. Up in smoke went his dreams of having Jeff on his team and the certainty of a winning season with a teammate his size.

Tryouts were scheduled for 10:00 Saturday morning. Timmy was up early, earlier than on a typical school day. It was a ten-minute ride to the park where tryouts were being held. Timmy was ready to go at 8:30, and the last hour of waiting seemed like an eternity. Earlier, Dad had decided to change the oil in his car. When he discovered that he had the wrong oil filter, he had to borrow Mom's car and go to the auto parts store to make an exchange for the right one. This set him behind a half-hour in his schedule. It wasn't until 9:55 that they exited the driveway. "Step on it, Dad," said Timmy.

"Don't get your shorts in a knot," Dad quipped. "These things never start on time. Besides, what's your hurry? You're not even trying out."

"Just wanna check out the new players."

As soon as they got to the field, Timmy jumped out of the car and ran to the field where tryouts were being held. He scanned the field, but just as he had thought, there was no sign of Jeff. *He must be really sick to miss tryouts,* thought Timmy. He did see Jeff's sister tossing a ball with several other kids in the outfield, so he ambled over to talk with her. "Hey Jess, where's your brother?"

"He stayed home."

"Still sick, huh?"

"Nah, he just was busy with other things."

And then it hit him like a ton of bricks. J. Billings! J. Billings from the list that Matt had shown him wasn't Jeff Billings at all; it was *Jessica* Billings! Jess was the one trying out. "You m-mean," Timmy stammered, "you ... actually ... play ... baseball?"

"No, silly, I'm here to take swimming lessons! How about you?" Dejectedly, Timmy mumbled something about already being on a team and sulked away. He walked toward the sidelines near the parking lot and watched as the coaches supervised the rotation of those who were trying out for a team assignment. *That girl's going nowhere*, thought Timmy.

Within minutes, Jess was rotated from taking ground balls at third base to the 'on deck' batting position. Timmy had watched her at third base. Nothing that was hit within reach got through her or by her, and she easily negotiated a very high pop fly about twenty feet behind her. Her limp was obvious, but it didn't seem to slow her down at all. She slowly walked in from third base and grabbed a bat from those supplied by the league, prompting Timmy to think, *This oughta be something else. She doesn't even have her own bat.*

And something else it was! It took only three pitches from the pitching machine. Jess stepped into the batter's box. First pitch, high and outside—*ping!*—over the right-field fence. Second pitch, right down the middle—*ping!*—over the center-field billboard. Third pitch, low inside—*ping!*—WAY over the left-field fence. Timmy stood in amazement. Only once in two years had he even come close to hitting one over the fence. The sudden silence in the park was deafening. Every head was turned her way.

Slowly there began a buzz as players quietly made comments amongst themselves, coaches grabbed notebooks and wrote notes, and parents exchanged glances and exclamations.

But Jess wasn't yet done. She slowly stepped to the other side of the plate and then, batting lefty, hit two more over the fence before smashing a line drive up the middle. *Exhibition over.* Jessica nonchalantly walked back to the bat rack, replaced the bat, took off her batting gloves, put them in her back pocket, and moved to her next station at first base.

The remainder of the morning was pretty routine, and by 11:30, tryouts were finished. Coaches would meet on Wednesday to complete the draft for the season. From what he saw, Timmy was pretty sure that Jess would be taken first in the draft, and that pick would go to the team that had finished the previous season in last place. That wasn't Timmy's team; they had finished last season with a respectable twelve and three record.

As Timmy walked to the parking area to meet up with his dad, he looked ahead and saw that he would walk right past Jess, who was talking with another girl who had participated in the tryouts. Never one to be bashful, he walked right up to Jess and gave her a high five.

"That was one awesome piece of hitting," Timmy said.

As she reached up to high five him back, one of her batting gloves fell from her back pocket.

It was a red Lizard Skins glove.

"Nice gloves," he exclaimed. "Where'd you get them?"

"Jeff gave them to me yesterday; it was a late get-well gift from my surgery a month ago."

And right then, the second light bulb of the day went off in Timmy's head! Everything suddenly came together and started making sense. When Mrs. Addison had introduced the twins to the class, Timmy remembered thinking that Jeff reminded him of someone. Then he remembered meeting Aaron when he bought the grip tape at Wadkins, and he now realized that Jeff must have been the one who had been down the street doing some window shopping. Could Jeff have been the one who stole the gloves?

"Earth to Timmy, earth to Timmy." Jess interrupted Timmy's thoughts. "Do you think I'll get drafted?"

"Is the Pope Catholic? Is water wet? For sure, I think that they'll probably skip over you as a player and just make you the league's hitting coach!" Turning toward the parking lot, Timmy saw that his dad was waiting. He looked back at Jess and said, "Hey, my dad's getting antsy; I'd like to talk with you more, but I'd better get going. Just for the record, I think you surprised everyone today; for sure, you surprised me." He smiled and bashfully continued, "Hope to see you Monday." *Now, why'd I even say that?* he wondered almost as fast as the words were out of his mouth. With that, he retreated to the car, having gained a whole different perspective on baseball, tryouts, and... and... on girls.

Later that evening, Timmy told his mom and dad about his encounter with Jess as he was leaving the park. Especially, he wanted to get their take on his suspicion that Jess's brother might be the one who stole the batting gloves. "What do you think I should do?" he asked.

"I don't think you should do anything," replied Mom, "until you pray about it and get some direction from the Lord."

"What makes you think that the Lord will talk with me?"

"Well, aren't you the one who thinks that you saw an angel? Since you believe that God would send you an angel, then you must trust that He will send you some thoughts and ideas.

Remember the story of David's son, Solomon? God had told him to 'ask for whatever you want Me to give you.' When Solomon asked for wisdom instead of wealth, riches, or honor, God was pleased with him and granted Solomon's wish. This might be a good time for you to ask the Lord for wisdom to do and say the right thing."

Dad suggested that they lift the situation in prayer. He led them in giving thanks for the angels, in seeking God's blessing on Jeff Billings, and in asking for wisdom for Timmy.

Pastor Remy's sermon on Sunday was about trust, specifically, about trusting in the Lord. He began with Proverbs 3:5, "Trust in the Lord with all your heart and lean not on your own understanding." As far as Timmy was concerned, he could have stopped right there. *Was he speaking to me?* wondered Timmy.

Pastor went on to say that one of the greatest struggles in life is the struggle to trust in God. He offered that trust in God is pretty easy when everything is going well, but the real challenge comes when life goes from the mountaintop of joy to the valley of despair. He posed this question: "How do you trust in the Lord when you don't know what to do?" The first bit of advice was "Wait. Bear in mind that our timing is different from God's timing."

Hmm, that's pretty much what Mom said last night, recalled Timmy.

And then Pastor mentioned four things to remember. "Remember," he said, "that God cares; He's with you; He's able to bring you through, and He's never not come through."

As anxious as he was to get this whole theft thing resolved, Timmy went home with a sense of peace, knowing that in some way, God, not he, would orchestrate a solution.

Sunday afternoon turned out to be a rematch in the wiffle ball arena. Timmy, Matt, and Dad held their own this time, and after two and a half hours, the game ended in a 6 - 6 tie.

Ecclesiastes 7:8

The end of a matter is better than its beginning, and patience is better than pride.

Chapter 9

God's Timing

Timmy awakened Monday morning and almost immediately was aware that something was different. The trouble was he didn't know what it was. He showered, dressed for school, and went into the kitchen for breakfast. Usually, in the morning, he awoke ready to devour the kitchen table, but on this particular morning, he pushed everything away. Timmy usually walked or rode his bike the half-mile to school, but Mom had agreed to an early shift in the hospital nursery that day and had told Timmy that she would drop him off at school on her way. This gave Timmy some extra time, but on this day, extra time was the last thing he needed. He was ready and waiting a half-hour before it would be time to leave.

"What on earth is going on with you?" asked his mom as he placed his bookbag by the door and paced back and forth, trying to make the time go by faster. He wasn't worried about school; he was an excellent student and never worried about school. He was just edgy, but he didn't even know why. The sooner he got to school, the sooner his day would begin and the sooner he would get to talk baseball with Jess. Jess? Was it the thought of baseball or the thought of Jess that made his heart race? Suddenly, she consumed his thinking. He heard her voice; he saw her smiling face. For some weird reason, he wanted to know more about her, her family, and her recent operation.

Timmy got to school ten minutes earlier than usual. He glanced around and saw that Jess was already there, but she was engaged in heavy girl-talk with three other girls. As he walked over to his assigned desk, Jeff approached him. "Hey, you're Timmy Dennison, right?"

"I am. What's up?" *Wow! Mom said to wait for God's direction. Is this it already?* he wondered.

"Mr. Wadkins suggested that I talk with you; probably won't have enough time now. Can we meet up during lunch?"

Unbelievable, thought Timmy. "Sure. I was actually hoping to get a chance to talk with you," he said curtly.

"OK, see you at lunch." Jeff turned and walked to his desk.

The morning couldn't go by fast enough. Timmy wasn't able to concentrate on schoolwork at all. As he thought about Jeff, he was having trouble controlling his anger and remembering all that Gram had told him about forgiveness.

By the time lunch rolled around, he was one ball of confused anticipation. Immediately after he sat down, Jeff came over and sat across from him. "I hear that you fly remote control helicopters," he began.

"I do fly once in a while." This wasn't the conversation Timmy had anticipated, and it threw him off his train of thought for a moment. "How'd you know?"

"Well, I fly a little, too. I mean, I don't yet, but I would like to. Before we moved, I lived near a town field that was used exclusively for flying RC stuff. A friend of mine got a new helo and gave me his old one. It was a beginner's model. Right after we moved, I went to Mr. Wadkins' store to order a few parts. Got to talkin' with him, and he told me that you and your Gramp did some flying."

What the heck are you doing, God? wondered Timmy. Nevertheless, he answered, "I used to fly with my Gramp, but unfortunately, he died a few months back, and I haven't flown much since. As a matter of fact, I picked up the helo for the first time about a week ago and ended up crashing it on Gram's roof."

"Sorry to hear about your Gramp. Anyway, I was wondering if maybe you could teach me a few skills, ya know, share some of your experience with me."

The time flew by as Timmy and Jeff continued their conversation about flying. Jeff seemed sincerely interested and was quite friendly. Timmy was aware of a "softening" on his part. In fact, he was beginning to see Jeff in a whole different light. When he looked up at the clock, he was surprised to see that the thirty-minute lunch period was almost over. He and Jeff agreed to resume their shared interest as soon as the opportunity presented itself, and he gathered up his books and trash. He was about to leave when Jeff said, "Oh, by the way, on the day that I ordered parts with Mr. Wadkins, I didn't get a chance to look around the store. Jess is always interested in baseball equipment. Does he carry that sort of stuff?"

"Sure, he does," answered Timmy.

"Well, a funny thing happened on the day that I ordered parts with Mr. Wadkins. I left the store and was headed to my mom's car a couple of blocks down the road when I noticed under the big blue mailbox a package of red batting gloves. I picked them up and looked them over. There was no identity or sales slip. I was gonna run back and see if they might have come from Mr. Wadkins's store when my mom yelled, 'Hurry up, Jeff. I'm going to be late for my hair appointment.' I tossed 'em on the back seat of the car and figured that I'd deal with them when I picked up my helo parts. After a couple of days went by, I sorta forgot about them until Jess saw them and kinda drooled over them. Probably, I was wrong, but I sorta lied and told her that I got them for her as a get-well gift as she recovered from her surgery."

God, You sure pulled that outta Your hat, thought Timmy. *Good thing I didn't go off half-cocked and accuse Jeff of stealing!* Recalling all the conversations with Gram, Mom, Dad, and Pastor Remy, Timmy was very much aware of how trusting in God's direction had worked out for the best. *Gee, Gramp, I didn't have to outmaneuver anything,* he thought. *I just let God do it for me!*

Timmy's mom picked him up right after school was out, so he didn't have a chance to re-connect with Jeff. He also never got a chance to talk with Jess, but he assumed that between school and baseball, he'd see more of her in the days and weeks to come. He still wondered who was responsible for the theft, but as the pieces of the puzzle fell into place, he realized that it might be something he'd never find out. And why should he? This was between God and the thief to resolve. Yet, he had a nagging feeling that there were still a few things he needed to address.

After dinner that evening, Timmy was able to corral his mom and dad, catch them up on the happenings of the day, share his opinions and feelings about what had transpired, and most importantly, get their views on where to go from here. Should he update Mr. Wadkins on everything he had discovered? Should he try to get Jeff to tell his sister the truth about the gift? Since the gloves were being used, should he try to persuade Jeff to offer Mr. Wadkins payment? Should he have another discussion with Miss Ludwig? Or should he let the whole thing just drop? As always, Mom and Dad patiently listened to their son's heart. Mostly their advice was as it had been before. *Maintain your faith and trust that God will lead you.*

Proverbs 23:23

Buy the truth and do not sell it - wisdom, instruction, and insight as well.

Chapter 10

Resolution

Tuesday evening, Timmy received a call from Mr. Wadkins, who told him that the helo parts he had ordered were in. Timmy said that he'd get there by the end of the week, but when Wednesday brought a warm, sunny spring day, Timmy got the OK from Mom to ride his bike to school so that he could pick up the parts after school. During the day, he had a few minutes to talk with Jeff; he offered to pick up Jeff's parts while he was at the store, but Jeff hadn't heard from Mr. Wadkins, so apparently, his order hadn't yet arrived.

When Timmy got to the store later that afternoon, there weren't any customers. Mr. Wadkins was busy behind the counter re-arranging one of the store displays. He looked up, recognized Timmy, and said, "Timmy Dennison, just the guy I wanted to see."

Oh, oh, thought Timmy, *I hope this isn't more trouble.*

"Your Gram was in yesterday. She wanted to surprise you and pay for the parts that you ordered. We got to talking about your latest helo mishap, and she told me about the mystery man, Gabe. Asked me if I knew anyone in town named Gabe who fit the description that she gave. She said that you thought this Gabe guy was an angel sent to rescue you. You know," he continued, "I'm not much on angels and church, but ... well ... come to the back of the store for a minute. I want to show you something." They negotiated through the aisles to the back of the store. Mr. Wadkins pointed to the back wall and said, "Do you see that black streak next to the breaker panel?"

Timmy looked. Not only was there a black streak next to the panel, but it also extended to the floor, where it traveled for about a foot toward the front door.

"I've only ever told this story to one person," Mr. Wadkins continued, "but seven years ago, when I moved my store into this building, I was replacing a broken circuit breaker when my screwdriver hit the bus bar in the panel, and I was knocked unconscious by a massive jolt of electricity. The next thing I knew, a young man was standing over me. 'I'm Gabriel,' the man said. 'I was walking by your storefront when I saw the flash of light. I came in to see if everything was all right and spied you lying on the floor, so I came back to see if I could help in any way.' My arm and my leg were burning hot as a stovepipe. Gabriel helped me to sit up and then to stand. As soon as he touched me to help me up, my arm and leg felt better. He only stayed for a few minutes, I guess just long enough to make sure I was OK. As he was leaving, he turned and advised, 'If I were you, I'd find an electrician to finish up that breaker replacement.' I hurriedly asked him if he had a business or home nearby, but he said that he was just passing through. For months after that, I checked out people in and around town, but I never saw the fella again. I've always felt that I owed that man my life."

Timmy listened to the story in awe. *Could it possibly be?* he wondered. Turning to Mr. Wadkins, he said, "My friend Pastor Remy would love to hear your story. I know you said you weren't much of a church guy, but Pastor Remy told me that sometimes when we run outta logical explanations, the only one that's left is a miracle. Besides, I think you'd like him. I'll meet you there some Sunday if you'd like."

Mr. Wadkins didn't reply; he seemed to be deep in thought as he walked back behind the counter and continued with his re-arranging. Timmy, too, was deep in thought. After a long moment of silence, he casually reached into his pocket and pulled out two ten-dollar bills and a five. He put the bills on the counter near the cash register.

"Whoa, wait a minute, son," said Mr. Wadkins, watching from behind the display case. "I told you that your Gram already paid for the helo parts."

"The money's not for the helo parts; it's for the stolen batting gloves."

"I thought you told me that you didn't steal them."

"Correct. I didn't steal them, Mr. W., and I don't know who did, but after a lot of thinking and praying and nudging, I'd like to square the debt. The guy who did steal the gloves is probably long gone, so for sure, he's not gonna pay you. Now, I think I know who ended up with them, and I think I know how it happened. The person who now has them probably doesn't even know they were stolen from you, so I don't guess they should pay for them. The person who found them lying on the ground under the mailbox didn't know that they were stolen from you, so technically, I'm thinking it's not up to them to pay. Now I suppose I could tell those people how I think that it all came about, but then that would ruin the whole thing that God has put together. For sure, you shouldn't take the loss. Otherwise, if it happened more often, you'd have to close the store, and us kids would lose the best sports supplier around. Now, the way I figure it, there's only one person left, and here's the thing ... in a couple of weeks' time, I've had to deal with being accused of stealing, I've made a couple of new friends, I've met an angel, I've learned about someone else who might have met an angel, and best of all, I'm about to get schooled on hitting by the best Little League prospect ever. All that is sure worth every penny of the twenty-five bucks. And besides, since Gram paid for my helo parts, I'm pretty flush with cash right about now. Everything fits. Can't beat that with a stick!"

Mr. Wadkins stood in amazement as he thought, *Where on earth did this kid come from?* After a long moment of silence, he finally spoke. "Timmy, you've made my day. Normally, I'd insist that you keep the money, but there's just something about your story that rings of clarity and truth. Wisdom is usually pretty easily recognized, but youthful wisdom like yours is rare; it is a gift that needs to be appreciated and honored."

Way to go, God, thought Timmy. He and Mr. Wadkins chatted for a few more minutes until Timmy looked at the clock on the wall and exclaimed, "I gotta get going, Mr. W. Thanks for getting my helo parts."

"It is I who should be thanking you."

Timmy grabbed the bag of new parts and was out the door in a flash; he grabbed his helmet from where he had hung it on his handlebars and was strapping it on when Mr. Wadkins appeared in the doorway.

"Hey Timmy," he called. With a big smile, he shouted, "How about you save me a seat in church next Sunday! It might just be time for me to talk *again* with Pastor Remy."

Timmy flashed a thumbs-up and was off.

As he peddled toward home, he reviewed in his mind the events of the past few weeks. He was aware of all the worries and fears that he had successfully negotiated (or, more accurately, the worries and fears that God had negotiated for him). He couldn't help but hear Gramp proclaiming, *I told you. Ya gotta outmaneuver 'em, my boy. Ya just gotta outmaneuver 'em.* Thanks to Gabe's interpretation, he now had a deeper sense of what Gramp's saying meant. He was pretty sure now that "outmaneuver 'em" meant seeking and following God's prompting for solving the problems in his life. He thought of his life as being like a huge jigsaw puzzle and imagined that God was sitting at a table, moving and changing all the pieces of his life until they fit together. And that vision made Mom's reminder of Romans 8:28 become ever so real.

He couldn't wait to tell Mom and Dad about his conversation with Mr. Wadkins and that Mr. Wadkins might meet up with them for church on Sunday. He was grateful that his faith and trust in God, along with the advice and suggestions from Mom, Dad, Pastor Remy, Gram, and Gabriel, had all combined to resolve his recent problems and predicaments. He was so deep in thought that he blew right by Gram's house. Out of the corner of his eye, he saw that her car was in the driveway, so he slammed on his brakes. Turning around, he rode up her driveway, dropped his bike on the ground, and barged in the back door. "Hey Gram," he shouted as he walked into the house. "Wait'll you hear how everything turned out!"

Gram came in from the den and, without a word, gave Timmy a big hug. It was a loving hug, a calming hug, a hug that told him how very important he was in her life. It was the hug that kept him coming back. Well, if truth be told, it was the hug *and* the fact that maybe, just maybe, Gram had on hand some just-outta-the-oven cookies that needed his loving and professional testing.

"Tell me all about it," said Gram ever so lovingly. "Pull up a chair for a few minutes and let me in on your story. It just so happens that a few minutes ago, I removed an angel food cake from the oven. First time I ever made one with this recipe, and I kinda think it might need some expert taste testing."

Acknowledgments

Many moons ago when I attended Fairfield University, I was unable to live on campus because I was also working a thirty-something hour-a-week job in Bridgeport. Consequently, I rented a room above the garage at the home of Mr. & Mrs. Robert McLevy and their two young boys. Mr. and Mrs. McLevy were wonderful people who gave me my space while often showing concern for my welfare. Several times in the years that I lived there, they came to my rescue. Many times during those years I recall Mr. McLevy calmly stepping back from a situation, lighting up his pipe, and proclaiming to no one in particular, "Ya gotta outmaneuver 'em." Thanks, Mr. M, for my title. That phrase, in addition to many fond memories of my years with the McLevy family, remains with me more than fifty years later.

My first book, *Timmy's Spiritual Christmas,* was dedicated to my eleven grandchildren and one (at the time) great-grandchild. Barrie Lamothe, the first-born grandchild, recently expressed an interest in trying her hand at cover design. I admit to a bit of caution before deciding on her diamond-in-the-rough talent. However, my decision to have her do the design was a rewarding one. Thanks, Pic, for a super job — better than I could have imagined. *Grampa's girl still does "tickle his heart."*

Once again, my sister, Carolyn Beaudin Hamada, has gifted me with her professional expertise in copy and content editing. This is a tedious and often overlooked job among the intricacies of writing. Thank you, Carolyn.

I am blessed with an abundance of families. There's the family to whom this book is dedicated; there's my birth family with whom I grew up; there's my extended family of "in-laws," "grands," "greats," etc., and there's my church family at BUMC. They have all supported the writing and publication of the Timmy book series. Indeed, each family is a "...gift that keeps on giving." Thank you, all.

Inscript Publishing continues to provide an avenue for Christian writers to get their works to the market. They offer affordable self-publishing services, including printing, binding, copy editing, cover design, interior design, and distribution of their books. Many thanks to Inscript's editorial staff.

Finally, I continue to be grateful to a faithful God, Who gifts me with the passion and persistence to bring meaningful Christian short stories to young and old alike. He gives me enough ideas and inspiration to proceed from chapter to chapter, the faith that He'll see the storyline to completion, and the trust that He'll use these stories to manifest His kingdom. Thank you, God.

www.ingramcontent.com/pod-product-compliance
Lightning Source LLC
Chambersburg PA
CBHW020524310726
48979CB00014B/2200/J
9781957497129